DON'T WORRY, LITTLE CRITTER ®

BY MERCER MAYER

RANDOM HOUSE 🏠 NEW YORK

LITTLE CRITTER, MERCER MAYER'S LITTLE CRITTER, and MERCER MAYER'S LITTLE CRITTER and LOGO are registered trademarks of Orchard House Licensing Company.

The material contained in this book was taken from the following publications: *I Was So Mad* book, characters, text, and images © 1983 by Mercer Mayer, and *Just a Mess* book, characters, text, and images © 1987 by Mercer Mayer.

All rights reserved. Published in the United States by Random House Children's Books, a division of Penguin Random House LLC, 1745 Broadway, New York, NY 10019, and in Canada by Penguin Random House Canada Limited, Toronto. The stories in this collection were originally published separately in the United States by Golden Books, an imprint of Random House Children's Books, in 1983 and 1987. Random House and the colophon are registered trademarks of Penguin Random House LLC.

Visit us on the Web!
randomhousekids.com
littlecritter.com

Educators and librarians, for a variety of teaching tools, visit us at
RHTeachersLibrarians.com

This special edition was printed for Target.

ISBN 978-0-375-97521-9

Printed in the United States of America
10 9 8 7 6 5 4 3 2 1

Random House Children's Books supports the First Amendment and celebrates the right to read.

I WAS SO MAD

BY
MERCER MAYER

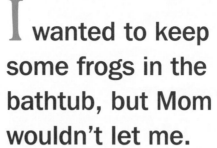

I wanted to keep some frogs in the bathtub, but Mom wouldn't let me.

I was so mad.

I wanted to play with my little sister's dollhouse, but Dad wouldn't let me.

I was so mad.

I was just so mad.

I wanted to water the garden,
but Grandpa said,
"No, you can't."

So I decided to decorate the house, but Grandpa said, "No, you can't do that, either."

Was I ever mad.

Dad said, "Why don't you play in the sandbox?"

I didn't want to do that.

Mom said, "Why don't you play on the slide?"

I didn't want to do that, either.
I was too mad.

I wanted to practice my
juggling show instead.

But Mom said, "No, you can't."

I wanted to tickle the goldfish, but Mom said, "Leave the goldfish alone."

"You won't let me do anything
I want to do," I said.
"I guess I'll run away."

That's how mad I was.

So I packed my wagon
with my favorite toys.

And I packed a bag of cookies to eat on the way.

Then I walked out the front door.
But my friends were going to the
park to play ball.
"Can you come, too?" they asked.

And Mom said I could.

I'll run away tomorrow if I'm still so mad.

JUST A MESS

BY
MERCER MAYER

Today I couldn't find my baseball mitt.

I looked in my tree house.

I looked under the back steps.

I asked Mom if she had seen it.
She said I should try my room.

I never thought to look there.
What a mess!

Mom said it was time
to clean my room.
So I asked her to help.

She said, "You made the mess,
so you can clean up the mess."

Dad was working in the yard.
He said he was too busy to help me.

My little sister said, "No way!"
And the baby didn't understand.

I just did it myself.

First, I put a few things in the closet.

I put my clothes
in the drawers.

I straightened up
my games.

I shut the lid
to my toy box

and put away
my books.

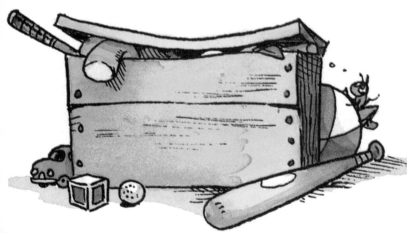

The rest of the mess could fit under my bed, so I put it there.

Then I made the bed.
Won't Mom be pleased.

I thought I might wash the floor.

But Mom said, "NO!"
So I just vacuumed instead.

Everything was just about perfect.

Then I noticed that my pillow was missing.

I looked on the other side of my bed,

and guess what I found?

My baseball mitt.